This book  to:

_____

TAILS FROM THE PANTRY

· Little Life Lessons from Mom and Dad ·

TAILS FROM THE PANTRY

Little Life Lessons from Mom and Dad

SOCCER

By Patsy Clairmont

Illustrated by Joni Oeltjenbruns

Tommy NELSON

www.tommynelson.com

A Division of Thomas Nelson, Inc.
www.ThomasNelson.com

Published in Nashville, Tennessee, by Tommy Nelson®, a Division of
Thomas Nelson, Inc.

Tommy Nelson books may be purchased in bulk for educational,
business, fundraising, or sales promotional use. For information,
please e-mail SpecialMarkets@ThomasNelson.com.

ISBN: 1-4003-0562-4

Printed in the United States of America
05 06 07 08 PHX 5 4 3 2 1

**This little series is dedicated to
Justin and Noah. . . .**

How blessed I am to have two "little mouse" grandsons who regularly nibble in my pantry. Darlings, leave all the crumbs you want in Nana's house. I'll tidy up later. Always heed Mommy and Daddy's lessons about staying safe. You are both loved "a bushel and a peck and a hug around the neck."

~Nana

*O*nce upon a jar of olives sat a mouse named Soccer MacKenzie. Yes, Soccer. His dad, Mac, named him after his favorite sport.

His mom, Lily, told Soccer, "Your dad almost named you after his favorite tool—a wrench."

Soccer thought about that for a minute and decided he really liked his name.

Soccer was practicing jumping, which is why he was perched atop the macaroni in the kitchen pantry. He had hopped onto a sardine can, then shot up onto the pork 'n' beans, and from there hoisted himself up the box of macaroni.

Once there, Soccer sat for a moment to catch his breath, and then as fast as he could, he ran right off the edge of the box. Down, down, down he tumbled, landing on a bag of marshmallows.

Soccer giggled so hard that he began to hiccup. His mom had taught him to hold his breath and count to ten when he had the hiccups. So he took a deep breath. . . .

One, two, three, four, five, six . . . was as high as Soccer could count without taking a breath. But it worked. His hiccups stopped. "Hooray!" Soccer shouted.

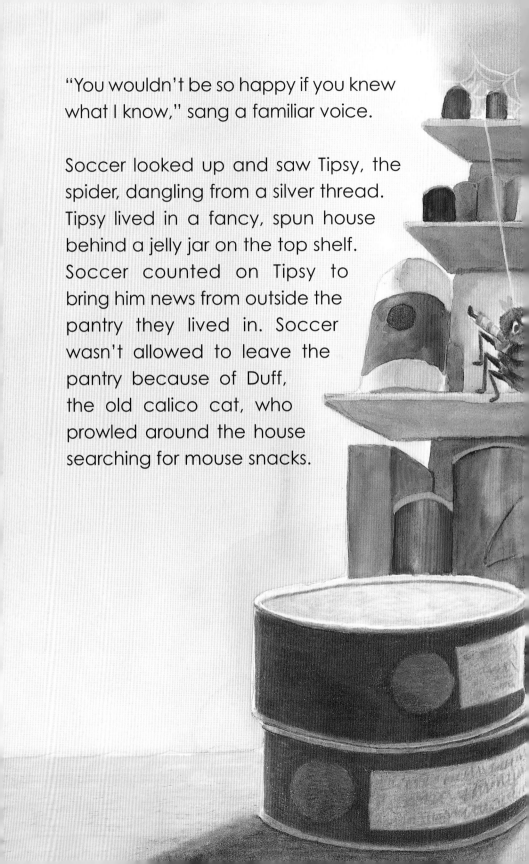

"You wouldn't be so happy if you knew what I know," sang a familiar voice.

Soccer looked up and saw Tipsy, the spider, dangling from a silver thread. Tipsy lived in a fancy, spun house behind a jelly jar on the top shelf. Soccer counted on Tipsy to bring him news from outside the pantry they lived in. Soccer wasn't allowed to leave the pantry because of Duff, the old calico cat, who prowled around the house searching for mouse snacks.

"What do you know that I don't know?"
Soccer asked.

"There's a new cat in the house!"
Tipsy announced.

"Is Duff gone?" Soccer asked, puzzled.

"Nooo, now there are TWO cats!"

"Oh my!" Soccer's eyes got really big.
"Two cats?"

"Yep, one, two . . . and guess what else? The
new one's name is Whomp, and I heard he's a
WILD cat."

"Whomp? Wild?" Soccer's knees wobbled. "Did you *see* Whomp?"

"No, Chatter, the ladybug, told me about him."

"Did Chatter see Whomp?"

"Uh . . . well, no, but she *heard* about him from Speck, the housefly, who saw him with her own seven eyes."

"I'd better go and tell my family," Soccer said, scrambling toward home.

Soccer lived in a forgotten box of Christmas candy with his family. Soccer's room was right next to a chocolate-covered caramel, which he loved to nibble on.

When Soccer got home, his mom was washing clothes. After hearing the news, she said, "Soccer, yes, we must be careful whenever we go out, but we also must be careful not to believe everything we hear."

Soccer was supposed to meet Tipsy in half an hour to play a game of checkers, but Soccer didn't know if he wanted to now. He felt scared. Wild cats are fierce and fast.

Then Soccer had an idea. He ran to his toy chest and pulled out his bike helmet, boxing gloves, winter boots, and wooden sword. After putting on his gear, he headed out to meet Tipsy.

Climbing was a bit difficult with boots and boxing gloves, but Soccer inched along carefully.
Suddenly, he tripped and fell backward, helmet
over boots . . . down, down, down, until he land-
ed on a sack of potatoes on the floor. Just then,
he heard a strange sound, and before he could
pick up his sword, a ball of fur with whiskers was
in his face.

"Eeeek!" shrieked Soccer.

"Eeeek!" shrieked the tiny ball of fur. And then
the fur ball began to hiccup. *HIC!*

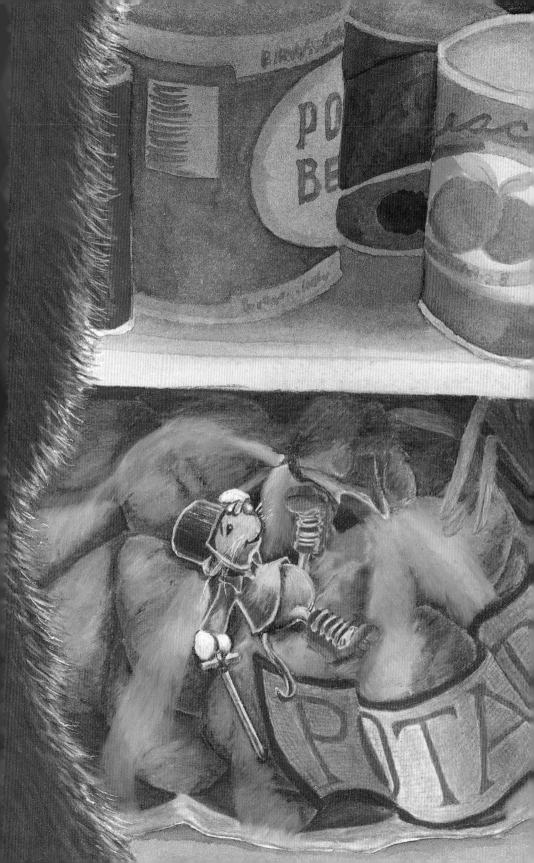

Soccer grabbed his sword and, shaking, yelled, "Who goes there?"

A little voice mewed, "My name is Whomp. Please—*HIC*—don't stick me with your sword."

"*You're* Whomp?" Soccer said. "You're a baby kitten!"

"I'm no baby! I'm just—*HIC*—small for my size. And you are a very oddly dressed mouse. Are you going to—*HIC*—hurt me?" Whomp asked.

"Uh, well, I suppose not. Are you going to smack me with your paw?" questioned Soccer.

"Oh, no, I don't like—*HIC*—hitting," confessed Whomp.

"Whomp," Soccer said as he carefully leaned toward the intruder, "if you hold your breath and count to ten your hiccups will go away."

"Really? Okay." Whomp counted until his cheeks filled with air—one, two, three—and then he gasped.

"My hiccups are gone. Wow! Thanks. Want to be friends?" Whomp asked.

"Friends? I will have to ask my parents about that, but thank you for offering. I have to go home now," Soccer announced.

Soccer took off his boots, tied the shoelaces together, threw the shoes over his shoulder, and dashed for home.

"Mom! Mom!" Soccer called as he ran in the front door. "I fell down and Whomp jumped at me. Whomp is a kitty. Just a baby, Mom. He's not wild at all. You were right. We can't believe everything we hear. Whomp wants to be friends. Can we, Mom? Can we?"

"Calm down, Soccer," his mom told him. "Friends with a cat?"

"He's just a kitty, and he doesn't like hitting."

"Hmm, we'll talk about this when Daddy gets home."

Just then the doorbell rang. It was Tipsy.

"I'm sorry I didn't make it for checkers, Tipsy," Soccer apologized.

"That's okay. I had a delay too," Tipsy admitted. "Chatter came by to say she had misunderstood Speck. Speck didn't say *wild* cat—she said *mild* cat. It turns out, Whomp's a quiet kitty."

"Well," Tipsy continued, "it's like my Aunt Centipede always says, 'You can't believe everything you hear.'"

Soccer just grinned.